Everything in Vero Beach was Eaten

Gage Irving

Everything in Vero Beach was Eaten
Copyright © 2024 Antoinette Beck
ISBN: 978-1-970153-51-4

No part of this publication may be reproduced or transmitted in any form or by any means, graphic, electronic, photocopy, recording, or by any information storage retrieval system — except for excerpts used for published review — without the written permission of the Author.

Maison
La Maison Publishing
Vero Beach, Florida
The Hibiscus City
lamaisonpublishing@gmail.com

"I... did... not... *cheat*! The coin was in the soup on the stove. I just followed the clues, that's all." Vince was adamant.

Cooper shook his head. "You have stories, Vinny; yes, you do."

Working for a moving company that flew thousands of tons of freight a year, 'D3 Spencer USA' was emblazoned in gold letters on the back of their dark blue uniforms. Currently on a job at the Miami International Airport, a jet had just lifted off; too loud to talk until the engine roar diminished.

Cooper was loading bales of cattle feed into two adjoining compartments on the transport plane with a forklift. Nine hundred pounds per bale, each one was twenty feet square, wrapped tight in heavy plastic. Each compartment could only hold ten bales, and he carefully anchored them on tracks installed on the steel floor. Air turbulence, or even a bumpy take-off or landing, would not toss this cargo around.

Ignoring orange warning arrows on the bales, the men didn't read the labels under those arrows either:

EXPERIMENTAL PROJECT
Livestock Feed rBGH\Rbst
IGF-IZ33

Inside the blocks were small pellets, a new food for cattle. Developed in a covert project in a restricted laboratory on the outskirts of Miami, the compound was supposed to make the cows grow faster and bigger. The creation was on its way to a cattle farm in Nebraska to see if the superfood actually worked.

Cooper was done with the installation on the second compartment. Vince stepped over and hit a button on a panel on the side of the jet to close and lock the door. The compartments automatically pressurize when the jet is airborne...but there was a problem he'd not noticed. A small bit of rope, part of the packing around the bales, got loose and it got stuck in the seal between the door and the body of the plane. This tiny interruption should not affect the pressurization; nevertheless, the connection was compromised, but Vince ignored the blinking red light on the panel. He and Cooper walked back to their lockers at the rear of the warehouse.

"Why are you limping, Vinny? Stick your foot under the wheel of a passing car last night?"

"I might have. I'm not sure where this ache comes from. I'm not up to my superhero strength." He moaned. "I need more coffee to get through the next job."

Cooper lightly punched his shoulder. "Winning those bar contests isn't helping you much at work, that's for sure."

Vince punched him back, and they laughed their way into the break room.

The warning light kept blinking before it shorted out an hour before liftoff, and the small corruption in the shield of the cargo door was not addressed. The information never reached the instrument panel in the cockpit.

Before turning inland to reach the Omaha Eppley Airfield in Nebraska, the pilot followed the coastline to avoid a line of heavy thunderstorms. His attempt failed, ending up in the flashing heart of a goliath. Pilot Bailey wrenched the yoke up to fly higher and get out of it. That didn't work either. Three lightning strikes hit the jet sequentially, following the skin of the craft before leaving through the end of a wing or maybe a tail rudder. These interactions usually don't damage anything of consequence on the plane, but the piece of rope in the seam gave one of the bolts a bridge into the compartment. A violent wrench raised the cargo door. The following sucking power of decompression bent the rails holding the bales down, and they flew out of the plane as wind-tossed dominoes.

Hotter than the surface of the sun, the bolt had also melted the heavy plastic bands holding the packing wrap around the bales. Outside the jet, they disintegrated as they tumbled in the wind. No longer controlled in the bales, small pellets fell on thirteen and half square miles of land populated by eighteen thousand residents of Vero Beach. No one had seen this invisible blanket covering their land in the lightless downpour. The residents in Vero got their lights back on at four that morning, and most stayed in bed.

The pilot saw a warning light. A compartment door was wide open, and he felt a shear against flying straight. He landed in Melbourne, only fifty miles north of Vero Beach, but the hatch had to be fixed. He called the company, telling them he was now only holding half the cargo. They told him to go to Nebraska anyway.

The heat of the sun evaporated the puddles, and the pellets glistened on the fields. Scientists had thickened the outer layer of these morsels to allow the cattle to use the rumen in their bellies to soften them before regurgitating them back into their mouths as cud. The temperatures and pressures during the storm removed the first layer, and that coincidence allowed other animals to eat them as well. These experimental balls lay in a yellowish wash across the acres. Any creature could partake in this heavenly manna.
But they didn't like the smell. Even the cattle ranging out there wouldn't touch them. The manufacturers will soon be upset when the surviving bales arrive at the testing site. Apparently, this accidental scattering of healthy food turned out to be pointless. It was inedible garbage. That odd situation appeared fine for the people of Vero.
There are fifteen hundred species of carnivorous geckos on planet Earth, and about twenty-two

varieties live in Vero Beach. The largest one is about fourteen inches in length.

Floridians see gecko lizards every day. They raced across the sidewalks or up a Palm Tree next to their front doors, yet no one noticed when the entire population vanished after that heavy lightning storm.

The cattle food was revolting to every animal — *besides geckos.* They found the experimental compound more than appetizing, and they licked, gnawed, and swallowed every single pellet they could find. When every single lizard belly was stuffed, it took three days to digest. Out of commission, they hid under leaves, boat ramps, or rusted-out cars, but most disappeared into the woods. Their eyes closed, they rested on their swollen torsos, burping and farting during an unusual assimilation mother nature had nothing to do with.

"Carl! Hey…Carl. Get out here! I need help to get this stuff set up!" Wendy was sweating hard as she held oversized paintings on top of her car, and her arm muscles were cramping. Her seven-year-old daughter had stepped out on the front steps of the house. Wendy looked over her shoulder. "Go back inside, Lisa. It's too hot out here."

She whined, "I need my phone. I can't reach it. It's on the top of the bureau, and I need to…"

"Shush. Go back inside and ask your brother to help you."

She frowned, but she did as she was told.

Wendy was beyond frustrated. He'd told her he'd run in and get the clips on the porch and come right back, but he'd been gone forever. Muscles letting go, she let the paintings slide off the roof. She slanted them against the hatch, and then she went inside.

"Where are you! Carl…come on. We need to get to the meeting."

What on earth had happened to him!

She opened the sliding glass door and entered the porch. Clips were scattered across the table and the floor. Outside in the yard, a cement bench had been tossed over, and a sneaker, just one sneaker, was left on the table. Her heart skipped a beat as irritation changed to worry and a touch of fear. Lisa had been wearing those sneakers when she saw her standing next to the front door a few minutes ago. Wendy ran inside the house.

"Lisa… LISA! Where are you?"

Virgil stumbled out of his bedroom, rubbing at his eyes.

"Have you seen your sister?"

"Why are you flipping out, Mom?"

Ignoring him, she ran up the stairs to Lisa's room. It was empty. She left the door open, hitting a number on her phone.

"Hello…Lydia? Things are getting weird over here." She was breathing too fast. "I need…ah…um…oh, oh…"

"Can I help you?"

"I can't find my husband or my daughter…and they were here a second ago. Oh, ah…aah…" Panic strangled her. "Get over here. I need help finding them!"

Lydia lived three blocks away, and she got there fast, parking off-kilter across her friend's driveway. Wendy shot out of the front door and hugged her.

"They aren't in the house, so…so they have to be in the woods." She waved in the air. "Back there somewhere."

"Okay, sweety. Relax. We'll find them."

Wendy began calling their names as Lydia followed her. Everything on the back porch was the same, but Virgil was now standing outside near the table and chairs at the edge of their property. The thick wall of trees behind him was moving like green clouds in a gentle breeze. He'd put the bench back up again, and he was holding his sister's left sneaker. Seeing Lydia and his mom on the porch, he waved.

"Hi, you guys. I can hear Dad and Lisa talking out there in the woods about a party. I'll go out there and bring them back!"

Virgil was thirteen. Five feet tall, his brown hair was razed short on the sides and longer on top. He wore shorts and a striped T-shirt, and he looked relaxed, but his expression changed. A scaley paw punched through the shrubbery behind him and circled his torso, embedding long claws into his flesh. It grabbed him, and he disappeared into the woods.

"*Oh my God!*" Wendy screamed.

"I'll call for help," Lydia said and dialed 911.

"What's your emergency?"

"A tongue came out of the grass…and, and then he disappeared!"

"Slow down. Tell me what you saw?" The operator was professional.

"Maybe it was fingers."

"I'm sorry, I don't understand. Please, tell me what is happening again?"

Wendy took the phone away from Lydia.

"My family is gone, and I don't know why. It could have been a snake or an alligator… or something else!"

"And two of you are still there?"

"Yeah, me and Lydia. Get somebody over here and help me find them!"

"What's your name and address?"

"I'm Wendy, Wendy Granger at 366 Palm Coral Lane. We need help right now."

"Officers are already on their way. It's important to stay on the line with me, okay? How much time has passed since they left?"

"Maybe half an hour, but Virgil was taken a moment ago!

"So, you have no idea what happened to them or where they might be?"

Wendy started to cry. She put the phone down and blew her nose.

"Wendy...hello." The operator was trying to get her back on the phone. "Are you alright...hello? Get back on the line with me, okay?"

Dropping the tissue, she grabbed the phone. "Yes... sorry. We think they're in the woods behind the house."

There was a long silence.

"Is everything all right...Wendy...talk to me, tell me what's going on. Hello, please! We need to stay on the phone until the deputies get there."

The emergency operator still heard nothing. Wendy had likely dropped her mobile phone...but then she heard screams moving farther and farther away from the receiver. The operator hung up and called back, but no one picked up.

Officers Kevin Shaw and John Dillon parked on Palm Coral Lane. A red hatchback had parked across the driveway of 366. Getting out of the cruiser, they looked unstoppable and heroic. Glock 17 handguns, cuffs, and other essentials on their belts and they also wore bulletproof vests. Responding with restraint, the deputies use fatal force only in self-defense or in deadly attacks on other citizens.

The door of the house was wide open. Shaw entered first, guard up. "Anyone here! Hello! Come back to me. We can help you."

Dillon was right behind him. They moved to opposite sides of the living room.

"I don't see or hear anyone," Shaw called to his partner. "Dispatch didn't tell us much. They could be in the backyard or in the woods."

"We need to check the house first… and be careful. I have a funny feeling there's something really wonky going on."

After searching the building, they stepped out on the porch. Blood was splattered on the tiled floor, and that spray ran all the way to the screen door. The concrete table and benches outside looked like a tornado had touched down. Wide red streaks dripped down one of the benches, and there was more red decoration on the top of the table… hanging in the branches of a nearby tree. The scene was beyond unsettling. Deputies Shaw and Dillon still looked powerful enough, but as they stared out at the barrier of trees, they felt uncomfortable; what had just happened might happen again any minute.

The last Friday of every month was slated for a public get-together in Vero Beach named 'Downtown Friday.' Five blocks on 14th Avenue, also called Main Street, was closed to traffic during the party.

Barriers were erected at the cross streets at 1:00 PM. Officers stationed at 20th St. and 14th Ave. redirected the traffic. The fest would begin at four, but the vendors needed time to set up their booths while town workers rolled in the portable stage. Food vendors at the event offered a plethora of items, from homemade ice cream and brownies to hotdogs and burgers. A local brewery even had reasonably priced wine or beer for the adults.

Orbital Keys was playing that night. They had two keyboard players for a lot of open-ended jams to evoke memories of the Grateful Dead. It was a larger crowd that Friday since some of their fans had driven in from Sebastian or Fort Pierce. These devotees, flowers woven into their graying hair, hoped to forget their day-to-day cares and float away on a musical cloud.

The music started with a rock classic with the audience clapping and swaying with enthusiasm. Isabel, their vocalist, belted the song out with gusto. The bass player and one of the keyboardists supported her with harmonies.

In their late fifties, Zach and Betty were standing near the stage. They loved the band. Zach hummed along until an odd-looking animal got on the stage. Its appearance silenced him with surprise.

"Betty, look! They must have paid a lot for a decoration that moves like that."

"I'll say...wait a minute. It's alive. Something is going wrong up there."

Isabel had tossed her tambourine in the air, and then she ran behind a speaker. A keyboardist got up so fast his instrument fell over. The gecko, the size of a Clydesdale horse, skittered to the edge of the stage. The frightening creature fanned out the thin scarlet dewlap under its chin in a rhythm of its own. The crowd hung between hilarity and shock as the remainder of the band members kept playing, momentarily unaware of a serious problem.

A second lizard, an Agama, had stamped up to the back of the stage, and he was part of the largest species of geckos in Indian River County. Redheads with black and red bands on their tails, their longest length had been about fourteen inches. But they'd eaten the tasty pellets, too. Now, they looked into the second-story windows of the nearby buildings.

Stopping behind the stage, the Agama nudged its snout under the platform, raising it high enough to break it down the middle. It shattered it into huge pieces. The drummer flew up in the air, and the audience reeled backward, any laughter replaced with screams. Towering over its easy destruction, the lizard stood up on its rear legs, front feet waving and cold black eyes hunting for a tasty prize. A keyboard player was pinned under a piece of steel from the canopy, and the Agama noticed him. Carefully stepping through this wreckage, the hungry creature easily reached the dazed musician. Opening a cavern with abnormally long teeth, the gecko lowered its head and swallowed the man—almost. It had left his leg behind, still pinned under the fallen canopy.

The size and density of the crowd at the party had released a powerful aroma. Any lizard smelling this tempting concentration was drawn to Downtown Friday. Many had congregated there, bellies grumbling, mouths open and drooling with excitement. Most of the partygoers were eaten. The few survivors had found an unlocked door or window and dove inside to cower.

Shaw and Dillon were on US1 when they got a call to go to 14th Avenue.

"Your wife and sister were supposedly to go there, weren't they?" Shaw said.

Dillon scowled. He sped up and turned 20th.

"Think positive, okay. They might have changed their minds… or left early."

Squealing around the corner, he stopped in front of the Auto Center on the other side of the barrier. The deputies got out of the cruiser. They just stood there. Gigantic lizards that looked like they came out of a Japanese movie from the sixties were eating people on 14th Ave. The smallest in that horde was seven feet in length, and the largest was about sixteen feet in the air. Dillon watched as a gecko broke a second-story window simply by jerking its head. The officers got back inside the car.

Their eating frenzy had been going on for a while. Not many people left, and their scaley feet slopped through widening puddles of blood. Tossing a head skyward, a lizard lassoed the noggin with its prehensile tongue, sucking it into its mouth like a cough drop. A smaller gecko pounded toward them, head snapping back and forth with a horrible bony click.

"What the hell is going on out there?" Shaw said.

"Hell, that's what."

The gecko planted its foot on the passenger window right next to Shaw's head.

"Put your head down, Shaw. I'll take care of this."

Dillon got out of the car. The gecko hissed back at him across the roof of the cruiser before he shot the creature in the eye. Falling to the pavement dead, Dillon got back inside the car.

"It would be suicidal for us to stay here any longer," Shaw said.

Dillon nodded and hit the gas. "I'm praying my family went home early. I called her and texted her, but so far, no one has answered."

"I pray they got out there in time."

Lizards wandered through Vero Beach, free to browse for meat. The deputies were driving back to the station, and they watched a middle-aged man on his front porch aim a shotgun at a gecko. He blew the monster's head right off, but it didn't save his life. An Agama rushed around the corner of his house and overpowered him.

Most of Dillon's attention had stayed on the road. However, Shaw looked back. The Agama had spit the shotgun out of its mouth, and it landed in a flower garden. It seemed that bone was one thing and gunmetal something else again. Likely too difficult for the gecko to swallow easily and digest.

Their captain had been hearing a lot of frightening accounts from his officers, and Dillon and Shaw's story about Downtown Friday turned out to be a cherry on top of a poisonous cake. The hundreds of people massacred at the festival on 14th Avenue had not been foreseen or controlled. Gigantic geckos attacking and eating whoever they saw continued, and he called his own section chief in Orlando. Vero was in peril, and it was beyond the power of local law enforcement to control. His plea for help echoed through the confusing corners of the bureaucratic system, but it did pick up attention. Six individuals eaten in a backyard had been recorded on someone's phone. It went viral. Soon, the entire world was captivated. The attacks were spreading, and the leaders of the National Guard in Fort Pierce were finally setting up a response. Be that as it may, a much more potent and faster source was about to respond with unstoppable force.

The horrible recording and more videos, just like it, reached General Hudson. Using his heavy connections, he went to work. He would stop the slaughter in Vero. Concerned that other geckos on the planet could also be affected, he called President Cadwell at midnight on the same day the Friday party in Vero Beach had become a slaughterhouse.

"Good evening, Mister President. I'm sorry to bother you this late, but the problem is important."

"Good evening, General. I know you're calling me for a very good reason. Update me."

"I don't know what the real percentage of loss of life in Vero Beach really is right now, but I do know it's getting worse. I think we need to handle this situation as fast...."

President Cadwell interrupted him. "We haven't done anything about it yet? Half the population could be gone by now!"

"I agree. The gravity of this emergency needs to be handled. Give me your permission, and I'll send troops in with the weaponry they need to eradicate the reptiles."

"I'll give you any authorization you need under these extraordinary circumstances."

"Thank you, President. That will speed things up. I'll send in a battalion of tanks to surround the infected area. The geckos can't get out of that area. With your say-so, I want to bring in flamethrowers. Haven't used them for years, but we've never quite faced an enemy like this one before. Fire should be an easy way to erase the problem. I have a connection with some paramilitary forces using the updated version, and I know they'll allow us to borrow a few. If that doesn't work, there are forgotten corners in our warehouses in Area 51 that also hold all sorts of things." The general chuckled.

"I told you; you have free reign. Get us the gear and help me save that city!"

"Yes, President, I will move on this as fast as I can."

"Update me, Hudson. Let me know when our forces are in Vero Beach."

Tanks encircled the city in a day and a half, and nothing and no one could pass that boundary. The United States Army Corps of Engineers had flattened a few buildings and cleared out some acres of heavily forested land to avoid any mysterious escapes. Their engineers had been careful. The walls of their cage were solid.

Gus had turned forty-two the week before, but his hair was mostly brown. The day before, he'd stood in front of his house on Deuce Court, right off 5th Street, with his brother. A lizard the size of a dinosaur had come out of nowhere and clamped Greg in its mouth. The monster disappeared down an alley at the end of the block, and Gus went back inside his house and locked the door. His station wagon was old but reliable. He knew it had gas. If an army of Godzillas had come to life, it was time to drive out of town.

He peered between the curtains. Since there were no geckos in his driveway snapping at the air, it was time to go. He took Route 60 to the interstate, and he'd drive I-95 as far north as he could go in one day. But when he got there, there were tanks in his way…couldn't reach the onramp. Gus rightly assumed they'd also blocked any other escape routes out of town. He parked near one of the tanks. Finding a few baseball-sized rocks, he began to throw them as hard as he could at the side of the tank and yelled out, "Hey! Hello, come out and talk to me! I want to leave. Get this damned thing out my way."

The hatch on top of the tank screeched open. The upper part of a soldier emerged, looking down at Gus. "Hey, hey, yourself. Relax. We're about to blow those oversized devils into pieces. Ground troops are on their way with FGM-14 Javelins."

"I have no idea what any of that means. Just let me out!"

The soldier's peaceful expression soured. "They're the best portable rockets we have. Remember bazookas? We stopped using them in 1945, and the javelins are the latest version. Some of the guys will have flamethrowers and others with M-14s. Those ugly giants out there will soon sing Sayonara."

"I don't believe you. Let me go."

"Sorry, sir, but I can't break this barrier. Look over your shoulder. You ain't the only one trying to get out."

Fifteen more cars had lined up, and thirty heavily armed individuals had simply walked there as well. Distracted, Gus hadn't noticed any of them.

The soldier ducked into the tank to reappear with a megaphone. "Listen...all of you, hold your horses." He was certainly loud enough to reach them. "Hundreds of men will get here and stop the geckos. Please turn around and go home and wait for the all-clear."

He looked down at them from his perch in the tank as they looked up, feeling hopeless. They didn't believe him any more than Gus had. The only escape they knew had just been taken away, but their devastation began to lift as transport trucks rolled off the highway in a thundering growl, lining up behind the tanks. Soldiers marched out of those transports, instantly working on their weapons and setting them comfortably on their backs. The uniformed men and women were soon ready for the lizard war. The number of cars parked on SR60 had reached forty-five. The drivers had gotten out, staring at the soldiers. Curiosity held them there.

The mutated geckos could smell the concentration of humans. A mass on them had formed on the east side of the intersection, Wawa on one side and the TA Travel Center with parking for 18-wheelers on the other.

For the soldiers, the upcoming fight with these behemoths looked simple and easy. Didn't have to find them. The scaley brutes began stamping straight at them, long tongues darting in and out of their mouths like grayish-pink snakes on meth.

The troops marched past the locals...who were no longer afraid, believing the geckos couldn't withstand an onslaught like this one. *Nothing could go wrong.*

The leaders of The Pink Legion, Melissa, and Caitlyn, sat in a cafeteria in the White House, discussing the future plans of the Legion. The group's objective was to balance human needs against an ecological balance. Yet they had not been tempered nor fair during most of their actions over their three-year existence. They believed that what we do on the planet is detrimental, and the majority of their triumphs had painful consequences.

Point in case: A building project in New Mexico was there to give the downtrodden their own homes. Local businesses matched government donations for enough capital for 'Step Up, Step Out' to buy a tract of land, and they would also set up low mortgages on these new residences. A boost many needed for a 'step up.' But it had gotten the Pink Legion's attention.

The group has scouts across the nation searching for injustices, and someone noticed a problem in New Mexico. The 'Step Up, Step Out' housing development owns sixty-five acres for the project. Orange Calla Squirrels lived on that land. The construction crews installing the water lines and the building foundations had found squirrels dead in their burrows, but what had actually killed the rodents had nothing to do with the building project. The Dekay River, a mile away, had flooded a week before the construction started, and that runoff left residue on the foliage the squirrels ate. That scum was lethal to Orange Calla Squirrels. Be that as it may, the project was still stopped by the energetic efforts of The Pink Legion.

The Legion's capital swelled with donations, and they were entrenched in most media outlets. *Doesn't everyone want to save the Arctic fox?* And the group had political clout as well, since Melissa was married to the president's brother.

The middle-aged ladies' discussion at the cafeteria lowered to whispers. They needed to find ingenious ways to ignite public fury over the outrageous slaughter of a new species in Vero Beach.

Melissa hissed across the table to Caitlyn, "Did you see the recordings I sent you?"

"Of course," Caitlyn whispered. "They're gunning them down in tortuous ways. I mean...I know they aren't supposed to kill people, but...but that's our fault! No one realizes this miraculous wonder is alive in Vero Beach. I think..."

Melissa cut in, "We'll save them! I'm going online after lunch to rally our members into action...and I'll call Frederick. Tell him about the danger those poor animals are in. No, no, they won't be on the extinct pile!"

"And I'll organize a demonstration," Caitlyn said. "Thousands will come to DC in twenty-four hours. We'll have heavenly support to save these miraculous arrivals!"

President Cadwell was alone in his office, frowning. He was stuck between a rock and a hard place, watching them march down Pennsylvania Avenue wearing pink. Some held down helium balloons that looked like friendly pink lizards. As the demonstration passed the White House, nightmarish creatures floated along, and the crowd below chanted slogans with religious dedication. Caldwell couldn't hear them, and he was happy about that, but the phone on his desk beckoned. *He did not want to make that call.* But the controlling power behind the Pink Legion had threatened his family and his political future if he didn't do what he told.

To get the military out of Vero Beach. The Pink Legion knew the geckos would be killed unless he stopped the assault. President Cadwell's body lowered in despair. He picked up the phone and ordered General Hudson to get the troops out of Vero while his soul cringed in shame.

The largest species of gecko in Vero Beach had red heads and red and black ringed tails, and they too, had merged in the wave of lizards slithering to the highway towards the troops. General Hudson had told Major Gordan to command the attack personally. Gordan sat in one of the transport trucks, overseeing the upcoming conflict through binoculars. At first, there was only a brownish-greenish blur of them, muscular legs pounding along. As the space between the troops and the hunger geckos shrank, Gordan fine-tuned the focus of his field glasses. Lizards were snapping at thin air with abnormally long and bloodied teeth. The horde hammered west, and the weight was so heavy the truck seat under him shook.

Major Gordan had done a little research on the geckos before their transformation. They never had regular teeth, just scales that had piled into conical nubs in their mouths. The unnatural and irregular modification had changed those nubs into fangs that had also grown thirty percent larger.

Gordan continued scanning the approaching group. An orange lizard with black spots and another with zebra stripes would have been fascinating if they weren't over seven feet tall. A bright green North American Anole was climbing the leg of an Agama that was twice its size. The smaller lizard reached the back of the giant, standing up there on its back legs, looking around. Its rose dewlap opened, indicating happiness. The Agama kept on rushing onwards to the soldiers, ignoring the weight of the Anole its back for a few minutes...and then it lost its patience. Twisting its head around, a blue tongue slipped out and lassoed the imprudent hitchhiker in a lightning-fast snap. Major Gordan watched the neon green Anole disappear inside the Agama's cavernous mouth.

Everyone who'd parked their vehicle on State Road Sixty got back in their car. The walkers asked a few of the drivers for succor, and they were invited inside as well. As the troops spread out across the fields and through the gas stations, it looked risky to be out there. An older guy tapped on Gus's window, and he'd let him in, introducing himself as Oliver. Since Gus was the first automobile to arrive, he'd already turned his jalopy around an hour ago. He wanted a better view of the fight, and as the soldiers waded into the geckos, all hell broke loose.

Oliver pointed. "Can you see that bonfire at the truck stop on the south side of 60? How'd they get those lizards into a pile... and make them stay on fire? Look, it's right next to the main entrance."

"I see it. A pillar of flames," Gus said. Then, he got utterly distracted. A soldier on the other side of the road fired his Javelin at an Agama. His shot was true, piercing the breast of the monster. And then the shell detonated, and the upper part of the beast exploded, flesh flying high before landing in a three-hundred-foot circle. The creature's legs and lower torso toppled over in the center of this blood-red target.

The soldiers realized the transformed animals could not match their firepower. Their nervousness was gone. They blew them up, shot them down, or burned them into kindling. The army would stay in Vero Beach until the menace to the citizens was eliminated.

Oliver had on a corduroy jacket and cotton slacks, long grey hair in a ponytail. "Looks like we're getting out of this thing in one piece after all." He'd rested his rifle between his legs, but he still looked out of place.

"What do you do for a living, Olly?" Gus said.

"I'm a professor at the Indian River State College. Of course, my future there doesn't look bright. It seems the troops are getting us out of this mess, but it's late in the game. We don't have a lot of supplies, and I'm worried about the hospital." He sighed. "Yesterday, I saw the manager of the Fresh and Fine Market ripped to shreds in the parking lot. Our day-to-day needs won't be handled easily…and no one knows for sure how this thing will actually end!"

Another soldier in the same gas station had aimed his Javelin at another gecko, but he hit a pump instead, and one of the main fuel tanks exploded, flames rising higher than the pyre of burning gecko bodies across SR 60.

Major Gordan had remained in the truck. The satellite phone he'd placed in a safe pocket in his uniform rang. He had good news for the General, and he smiled as he answered that call.

"Hello."

"Stop the advance."

"What? We're overpowering the geckos, and they are…."

"I order you to stop the advance. Retreat now!" General Hudson ended that call abruptly. He gave him no explanation, not even a goodbye.

The Major wanted to call the General back or just rebel from the order, but he knew his own feelings had no power. He sent out a stop and desist to the eight captains in the field, even though he knew that following that order would slaughter more innocent people. Gordan knew they could hear his orders in their earbuds, many distorted in the noise of battle, but it would reach them all eventually. In twenty minutes, all of the officers had accepted their order. It hadn't made any sense to them either.

The full withdrawal was not easy, quick, or gentle. The ravenous lizards kept attacking with ongoing fatal consequences for them. The men kept using their weaponry during the retreat. Having already killed sixty percent of this pack of lizards, they couldn't understand why they'd been ordered to leave. The lizards would keep hunting people throughout the city if they weren't stopped. The columns of flames on either side of the main road looked like exclamation points, underlining the absurdity of their withdrawal.

Gus was pale. "The troops are leaving."

"Why are they leaving?" There was dread in Oliver's voice. "The problem is not resolved. This is wrong."

"More like *warped*." Gus stepped out of the car. "I'll talk to the guy in the tank again, ask him what's happening. Make him change his mind, or at least let us get on the highway and leave!"

"Stop, Gus...*stop*! We have no time. We need to get out of here. When the soldiers are out of their reach, they'll turn on *us*."

Gus quickly understood that warning, and he got back into the car. "You're right. We'll be their next target. Our cars aren't strong enough to withstand that attack, and we also don't have the firepower. Getting out may be the only option we have."

Gus started the engine, and he left tracks in the grass as he veered onto State Road 60 in a hurry. Leaving the long line of parked cars still facing west behind, no one else seemed to realize what was about to happen. When the last of the soldiers got behind the tanks, a gecko tried to get through the barrier to reach them, but it was instantly killed by a heavy barrage of high-caliber bullets coming from one of the tanks.

At that point, the lizards redirected their attention toward the humans hiding in their metal shells close by. Realizing the position they were in, watching the monsters move towards them, they finally started their engines in a frantic escape, making U-turns at the same time.

"How are things going back there, Olly?"

"Not good."

"I can't look around. What's happening?"

"Be grateful the geckos aren't on *us* right now," Oliver said, and then he groaned. "I'm taking a photo. You can see it when you stop driving--*if you want to.*"

In their panicked escape from the gecko's approach, their driving abilities were skewed by fear. Using both sides of the road, many reached over sixty miles an hour. The driver of a Mustang swerved around a Civic, clipping the smaller car's front bumper. The Civic slid into the side of a Ford Econoline which flipped over on its side, an instant roadblock. A Corolla hit one side of the tipped-over van, while a Toyota Tacoma bounced off the other one. Other cars tried to avoid the Econoline, which triggered more crashes. Everyone's attempt to escape from the geckos evolved into a demolition derby with no audience and a winning prize sending you to heaven.

The derby didn't go on for long. The lizards waded in on acres of stationary cars holding nuggets of tasty morsels. Gus and Oliver had gotten out of there just in time. Three people were killed in the crashes, and many were injured and unable to walk. Only eight individuals made it through this mayhem, finally speeding away on the state road.

Major Gordan was crying. Looking through his binoculars, he saw what was happening to the people left at the entrance to I-95. The Pink Legion was behind this illogical retreat, but he didn't know that. He didn't know they'd cornered his president with a force powerful enough to direct him. *Just as well.*

Indian River Mall had become the last refuge. Deputies Shaw and Dillon were busy transporting necessary items over there inside a mail truck. Dropping off pallets of toilet paper, food, and medical supplies, they were about to go for more when Captain Ethan's voice crackled to life on the radio.

"I know Army troops had arrived on SR 60 a few hours ago, but they've left. Something went badly wrong. The few survivors that had driven up there are now driving east on 60. Go out there and flag them down at 66th. Get them over here. Lizards are breaking into office buildings and homes now. It's difficult to get away from them. Take a cruiser over there and use the warning lights to get their attention as they drive past."

"Will do, Captain," Dillon said.

After changing vehicles, they picked up the handmade sign about shelter and security. Reaching the intersection of SR 60 and 66th Ave., they turned the car lights on, and Shaw put the sign against the telephone pole, holding it there with a rock. Gus and Oliver were the first to stop.

"A few more cars are coming," Gus told the officers. "We tried to get on the interstate, but army tanks were in the way. After they left, the geckos attacked us."

"I advise you to get off the highway and go to the mall," Deputy Shaw said.

"There aren't a lot of options left. I have no groceries at the house, and I can't fight back by myself anymore...yeah, okay. We'll go over there. Thanks," Gus said.

The officers directed anyone who'd stopped to go to the only sanctuary left in town. Most took their advice. However, the cars stopped coming. In the distance, the horde of geckos they'd heard about was moving towards them on the highway, and they were getting closer fast.

"Time to get out of here," Dillon said.

"Okay...wait a second. We should get to your house. See what's up with your wife and sister!"

"You're right. I think we can squeeze that in. Let's go." Dillon had been upset when he lost his phone connection with his wife.

Taking 66th south, they had avoided the lizards. They reached his house in less than ten minutes, and

Dillon leaped out of the cruiser and ran through the unlocked front door. No one was inside, and he ran through the back door and into the yard. Their small personal bags holding their phones and wallets were left on the edge of the canal. That was an ominous sign. That part of the canal was too narrow for most boats. Dillon was even more confused and upset, and he kneeled to open their bags to see if their phones had been left behind.

Deputy Shaw walked into the backyard to see his friend and partner motionless, staring out into space. Shaw spoke to him softly. "The captain just called, ordering us back to the mall. More people have arrived, and he wants us to help coordinate things."

Dillon stood up, holding their bags. "It looks like…" He stopped and breathed out and started again. "I can't figure this out. At least there aren't any pieces of them around. May have left their stuff behind for a reason, even if I can't figure out what it is."

Shaw tried to help. "If Geckos had been here, their bags wouldn't be sitting there. They'd be…" He ended that painful description, hurrying on. "There's nothing we can do here, and they need us at the mall."

"I'll leave their bags here and…" He grabbed a piece of scratch paper out of his pocket: *'Riley, I will be at the mall off 60. Call me or get over here! Love, John.'*

He left the note in his wife's pocketbook and lowered his sunglasses to hide his eyes. His voice was cracking up a little bit.

"You're right, Shaw. We gotta go back. I have a bad feeling things will get worse before they get better."

The deputies entered the mall, and another officer guarding the entrance directed them to the north side of the building.

"About time you got back!" Captain Mello greeted them. "They're crashing through windows now. That's why more people are showing up. We're boarding up all the exits besides the main one, and we'll watch that entrance carefully… with a lot of gunpowder."

4x8 sheets of plywood were resting near the entrance of a bookshop. "Shaw, get over here," Mello said as he grabbed one of the boards. "Take the other side!"

"Yes, sir!"

Dillon had taken his jacket off and tossed it on a nearby bench. "I'm good with a hammer too, Captain. Maybe I should help Randy at one of the other exits?"

"Good idea. Go for it!"

The mall had become a last-ditch sanctuary without the government support they needed. Giving newcomers cots and general directions, they used the commercial ovens to cook communal meals and feed the growing crowd. They intended to hand on, dig in, and survive.

Deputy Dillon's wife, Riley, and his sister, Cassandra, had stayed at the Downtown Friday party for thirty minutes before Riley got a call from their next-door neighbor. He'd fallen, and he couldn't stand up. The women left downtown to help him, an action that likely saved their lives.

When Henry opened the door, he was healthy as a horse.

"You don't need our help at all!" Riley was stunned.

"Sorry. The situation around me is more broken than my old body. It's getting deadly to stay here. Follow me to the second floor and see for yourselves!"

As the geckos overpowered the crowd at the party downtown, another pack surrounded the hospital. The smell of blood from surgeries leaked out of the AC vents on the walls of the building. A potent lure, the lizards were drawn there.

Henry and Riley lived only four acres away. Henry could see the entire medical property from his bedroom. A gecko had broken the doors of the main entrance into the hospital with its tail. Safety glass was scattered across the lobby, and other lizards smashed in patients' windows...at least the lower ones and the ones under ten feet in height had gotten inside the reception area.

A small percentage of this large group turned away from the hospital, pounding over the bridge that connected the hospital property to Graceful Fields, a residential community. It was only a mile away from

Cranberry Villa Road. The pack would arrive at their door in twenty minutes.

Henry turned away from the window. "We need to get out of here fast. My cousin has a place for us on her boat docked at one of her houses."

"How can we get there?" Cassandra asked.

"My landscaper got my paddle boat out of the garage and into the canal for me an hour ago. We can escape on that."

"Why don't we just drive? We got here from Main Street with no problems."

"It's not safe out there anymore. I looked at the live feed on the local news channel. You'd be in way too much danger driving. There's only room for one on my boat, but you can hold onto the safety bar at the stern. I'll hold your bags on my lap so they'll stay dry. Just get in the water and kick. We have to get out!"

Riley followed the others down the stairs, scowling. She couldn't reach her husband on the phone. Reaching the canal, Henry settled himself in the seat. The pedals were set up in a simple system, transferring the power under the deck to the paddle at the front of the craft. The deck and the paddler stayed dry.

The women stripped to their panties and bras and tied their clothes on a side rail. They'd left their handbags on the grass next to the water's edge. They were about to pick them up and give them to Henry before jumping into the canal.

Seven Brown Anole Geckos raced around the corner of the house. Their dewlaps were usually reddish orange, but those fleshy flags had darkened to black. A warning when they get aggressive. Seeing the hungry glimmer in those eyes, Cassandra and Riley leaped into the water and grabbed the back rail of the paddleboat, kicking as fast as they could. Riley yelled out to Henry, "Paddle harder!"

"I can't push any harder, damn it," Henry shouted back. The boat was actually moving speedily enough away from lizards snapping their jaws in frustration.

"How long before we reach her dock?" Cassandra's question was harder to hear, weakened from the close encounter.

"An hour, maybe. It's less than two miles. Hard to know for sure, and I'm not sure exactly what the tide is doing right now."

Riley's other neighbor, Hildegard, hadn't been keeping up on the sudden intrusion of geckos. Drawn into her backyard by the strange noises the Anoles were making out there, there was a good chance some of the lizards would have jumped into the water after the two women, hunger overpowering their aversion to water. Her sudden appearance redirected their attention, and there was no swimming involved.

Hildegard hadn't had time to go back inside her house. She stared at the small group of geckos in shock and awe before the leading Brown Anole clamped its jaws on her leg, and the next one sank its teeth into her neck, black dewlap jiggling. Swallowing Hildegard down their gullets, the Anoles ran onwards, hunting for more. They'd forgotten about the paddle boat, and it was out of sight anyway. The handbags were left untouched on the grass.

Riley relaxed in a back cabin inside the *Humdinger*, a forty-five-foot-long yacht.

"The geckos never went on the dock when they were small," Riley said. "And now they'd just break through the boards and fall into the water."

Cassandra sighed. "Thank God, we made it. And Henry's cousin is allowing us to stay here, a nice thing to do."

"Her name is Terri," Riley said as she got off the cot. "Henry forgot his phone when he left his house in that crazy dash, so I'll just ask her if I can borrow hers." She climbed the four steps out of the cabin. "I'm going on the deck."

Riley was surprised that the cushy chair she sat down on was boat furniture. Cassandra had followed her up.

"It's a blessing we're still alive," Riley said. "We have to accept what we have, breath in clear air in a fairly safe place."

"Yeah, but…" Cassandra paused, nervous about her answer to her. "But we're in a trap, and there seems to be no way out of this. We need to figure out what's going on and how to fight back... and then get the hell out."

Riley stared at her. "And how would you have us do that? We have no communication or any weapons. Right now, we can only..."

Henry stepped onto the boat and put his bags on the anchored table. "I found four family servings of bourbon chicken and rice in the freezer in the cottage. We can use the microwave in the galley and heat them right up."

"Great," Cassandra said, and then she waved. "Terri's coming onboard."

Red-headed and tall and dressed to the nines, her sling-back high heels somehow hadn't gotten stuck in a crack on the dock. She moved up the ramp onto the boat with serious intent, eyes stormy, red lips in a straight line.

"Hello, Terri. Nice to see you." But Henry was confused by her demeanor. "Something wrong?"

"A lot is wrong, you dolt." Terri's voice had a razor's edge. "Geckos are eating us, and that's not a lot of fun." She stamped her three-thousand-dollar Jimmy Choo shoe on the deck of her boat. The sound echoed. "I have no idea how bad this will be." She glanced at her female guests, and her scowl deepened.

With no other options, Riley smiled and reached out to shake her hand. "Hello, Terri. I ran past you when we first got here. We haven't met yet. We both appreciate your help on our--"

Terri kept on talking to Henry as if Riley wasn't there....

"You've supported me through financial ups and downs over the years. That's why I accepted your neighbors to stay on my boat, but something came up. Tiffany's on her way since lizards destroyed her home in Sunset Landing in the Callejon district, just a few miles south of us. She and her two children will stay on the *Humdinger* with you. Your friends must leave asap."

"Hold on, wait a minute, Terri. Cassandra and Riley have no place to go. You're throwing them to the wolves. Why can't Tiffany stay with you in the main house?"

"There's no more space left, I'm sorry about that." Her apology sounded flat as a pancake under the wheel of 'I don't give a damn,' and her last statement only included painful information. "Tiffany will be here by seven."

Turning gracefully on her high heels, Terri sailed towards her golden throne, wherever that might be.

Cassandra cried out, "Wait! That can't be right. We need to stay together. Riley and I can fit into anything. We might get killed out there! *Pleeeease... wait!*"

The queen waved over her shoulder, deaf to her heart-wrenching wail. Cassandra crouched on a bench at the edge of the deck and began to cry. Riley looked over at her and then she sent daggers at Henry with her eyes.

He cringed. "I don't know what to say or what I can tell you to do, but...."

Riley interrupted him, "Terri is your cousin, and you're family to her. She's helping *you*; I don't think she understands any other concept. We have nothing but the clothes on our backs. Oh yeah, we're in great shape! No guns, no phones, and nowhere to go. How can we survive?"

Henry sat next to Cassandra and held her hand. Riley walked up close to him. "Leave her alone, Henry. Give her some space."

And Henry instantly got up. Riley went on, "Tiffany will be here in a few hours, so we need to find a way out of here. Your landscaper said there are survivors at the Indian River Mall, right?"

"Yup." Henry perked up. "There's a way to get you partly there!"

"Your paddle boat. If you let us use it, we can get back to my house. Maybe there won't be any geckos when we get there." Under more pressure, she started to shake, and she breathed deeper to calm down. "We'll get guns at my house and take Cassandra's car over to the mall."

"You can certainly use my boat. I can't believe she's put you in this position." Anger flashed across his face. "If she'd done that to *me*, I'd--" He stopped. That subject was inappropriate... "Yes, taking the paddle boat is a good idea, Riley."

Cassandra realized she was about to fight the odds—no more crying or whining. And it was almost 2 PM. "I don't know if geckos move around at night or not, but if they do, darkness might be worse for us.

Let's use the daylight we have left and get to the mall. I think our families and friends are likely there too."

"I agree with you, Cassandra." Riley scowled over at Henry one more time. "There's nothing for us here."

They'd found a simple way to get both of them on the small boat at the same time. Riley would paddle while Cassandra squeezed behind the seat. The journey along the canal remained calm for a while.

Riley pointed. "Look! It's swimming with us."

"Good God!"

The alligator was fourteen feet long, and its back was crisscrossed with greyish-brown scars. Something must have sliced through that bony-plated hide years ago. The creature submerged, and the paddle boat wobbled back and forth.

"We have nothing to fight it with!" Riley yelled.

The starboard side of the bow rose. Leaning over the rail, the two women saw a black eye just below the surface, and it looked straight back, but only for a minute. The gator opened its jaws to reveal a long tongue and endless teeth even as the bow got higher in the air. Suddenly, the craft lurched forward and landed flat on the surface again. The creature had disappeared, the surface calm, not a ripple.

"Do you think it's gone?" Cassandra asked.

"I don't think so."

It was the stern this time, and they held the seat back. The slant got crazy steep fast. Either they'd fall off the deck, or the paddleboat itself would just flip over.

On the other side of the channel, two Nutrias, an invasive rodent, were tussling on a tree branch hanging right over the water. Twenty pounds apiece, their battle threw them into the canal, but they kept on scrapping. The loud slaps of their feet reflected their wild energy.

The paddleboat dropped even harder this time, but their grip on the seat *and* the wheel held them on the deck. The alligator shot out from under the hull and surged across that short expanse, jaws wide open. The plump Nutrias were enveloped. The creature closed its maw in a snap, disappearing under the surface. Serene on the canal again, this time they thought the Nutrias had taken their place and the peace would remain.

"We almost got killed." Cassandra's voice was faint.

"A good force saved us. Those animals were sent here as a godsend, no lucky coincidence involved."

Riley paddled again, with her sister-in-law crowded in behind her. They reached the house in an hour and a half. No more surprises. Cassandra tossed a rope around a pylon, and Riley hopped out. They were both relieved their bags were still there, and Riley quickly found his note.

"*Riley. I'm at the mall. Get over here! Love, John.*" Casandra read it over her shoulder.

"He's alive! Kevin must be with him, too." Cassandra was elated.

"This is a relief." Riley tried to call her husband again, but still no answer. "We need to get there. I'm going to get the bottles of water and the guns out of the safe." That note got her in high gear. She jogged to the house and back with the items in under ten minutes.

She tossed the case of water in the back seat, leaving the three guns on the floor in front of her feet. Cassandra started the car.

Riley looked at the dashboard, "Not much gas in the tank, Cassie, and I don't think the stations are open anymore."

"There's enough!" Cassandra frowned. "And it's only five miles away."

"Why'd you buy this old Mustang?" Riley tilted her head. "It's dragging you to the poor house. I think...."

"I think it's one of a kind, and it runs perfectly. On a good day, I'll vex you in your Lexus in a cloud of my classic dust!"

Riley laughed until a gecko ran up close, trying to reach the car. Grabbing a gun, she lowered the passenger window and shot straight at the heaving monster racing along behind them.

"Hit the gas we got, Cass. Gotten leave this thing behind."

Riley's bullet had only grazed this Tokay Gecko, but at least the spotted hulk was faltering. Cassandra hit the gas, and they left the fiend behind.

"It's ain't easy out here," Riley said. "We have to get to the mall."

Against her expanded worries, no other geckos showed up.

Shaw and Dillon were on guard duty at the only working entrance. The parking lot spread out in front of them, and after that, the road that circled the entire plaza. Shaw noticed lumps piled up against the wall of a closed business on the other side of that road.

"Dillon, can you make out what that is against the wall of the tire shop?"

"Not sure. Maybe leftover supplies were dropped off and forgotten about after the attacks. Hold on. Larry has binoculars. I know he's moving rice and corn into the cooler. I'll just go inside and borrow them."

Quickly reappearing, he looked through the glasses and groaned. "It's four of them, and one is an Agama."

"Maybe we should ignore them right now, but after sunset, we can blind them with a spotlight. We could shoot them before they get their sight back."

"Sounds good, but we should use two cruisers and more guys."

Shaw borrowed the binoculars to see the latest tribulation in a clear and precise vision that seemed to have come out of a nightmare.

The Cobra's engine coughed, and Riley felt uneasy. They were close. So close. Taking the entrance into the shopping complex, they stayed on the outside road. Passing Best Buy, they'd park next to the entrance of the mall and run inside.

"I haven't seen any lizards since the one you shot near the house, and we'll be in the safest place in town soon." Cassandra smiled, even as she pumped the gas pedal with sweat breaking out on her forehead.

And Riley was pale. The trip was not over yet. This last inch could be a hurdle, and then the engine died, and the Mustang rolled to a stop. She looked across the lot. The entrance was close, just six hundred feet away; however, their senses had been dulled by exhaustion. Four geckos slept against the side wall of the tire store across the road, but they were blind to that serious problem.

"Here, Cassie." Riley gave her the nine-millimeter Glock. She'd take the AR-15. "We have a good chance to make it to that entrance in one piece. I don't see any geckos anywhere, and now we can defend ourselves. You remember everything you learned in the classes your brother picked out for you last year, right?"

"I won an award for my marksmanship! If I see one, I'll take it down." Cassandra giggled, but a nervous tickle at the back of her throat silenced that. "God is on our side."

"Nothing will stop us!"

Opening the doors, they raced towards the mall, guns at the ready.

Shaw and Dillon watched the Mustang stop at the far edge of the lot. The women quickly burst out of the Cobra, clearly unaware that lizards, scales now glowing orange from the setting sun, were running up behind them. As the behemoths closed the gap, the deputies realized who those ladies were. They couldn't get there in time to save them, but they ran as fast as they could, nonetheless.

The Agama encircled Riley's waist with its long tongue, and she lost her grip on the gun in a lift off the ground. She hadn't had enough time to fight back. The rifle fell to the concrete with a muffled clunk, and she rose higher. The lizard was pulling Riley into its gullet with a relaxed enjoyment. Drool pooled in its mouth and dribbled to the pavement below.

Another gecko, taller than a grizzly bear, tossed Cassandra to the pavement with a clawed foot. The monster lifted its front paw to rip her left arm off and swallow it. However, another in the group interrupted that act. It wanted the succulent prize for itself, and a short battle ensued. The lizard, holding her down, swept the same front paw across the throat of the intruder, claws tearing into the attacker's flesh. Blood splattered on Cassandra's face, and the injured thief-to-be reeled back and slunk away.

Riley squeezed, and Cassandra pinned. Neither could see nor react to the next interruption, but the deputies stopped running and looked up. So did the geckos, tilting their heads at the fast-moving copters flying straight at them. Four helicopters had risen over the roof of the mall like a magic trick as if they'd come out of nowhere.

A few miles out, the pilots had switched on the camouflage effects. It lowered the engine noise by retracting some rotor blades inside tubes that were part of the lift system. They also used a secondary effect, realigning the soundwaves from the engines to go out of sync. When they reached the mall, they turned the buffers off for a sudden blow of decibels and visual surprise for anything or anyone on the ground.

Jaws open in fury and confusion, the geckos snapped at the copters' landing skids hovering just out of reach. The side doors of these aircraft opened to reveal men wearing olive-colored uniforms perched on metal stools welded to the floor. The men aimed unusual guns at the heads of the reptiles. These guns had bluish spheres the size of Christmas ornaments attached to the end of those barrels, and they emitted a ray deeply absorbed into their brains. The geckos sank to the asphalt as if they'd been put to sleep with a tranquilizer, but it was a lot more than that. They were still alive, but they'd never wake up again. A permanent coma.

Distracted by the helicopters' arrival, the Agama let Riley go. To avoid a nasty fall, she sank her fingernails into the gecko's tongue and held on. The Agama pulled the muscular organ back inside its mouth even as it slumped to the ground. Riley let go just in time, not wanting to be sucked inside its mouth either. She climbed over the gecko's upper lip and onto its snout. From there, she walked the length of the lizard's body and then on the tail. It got low enough for her to finally jump off.

In Cassandra's case, the lizard's foot moved to the left when it fell. She wriggled out and ran to the mall.

Looking back, she saw Riley standing next to the biggest one of the group, picking at her hands. Cassie changed her direction towards her instead.

The men in the foreign helicopters were done with what they had intended to do to those geckos. They turned south to hunt down more. There were more copters fitted exactly like they were, flying over other sections of Vero Beach with the same intention. The deputies began running to Cassandra and Riley again.

The Agama's snore, a nasty wind, pushed Riley forward while she jumped off the tail that had curved in front of its face. Stepping away from this lump, she shook herself and looked back at the tire shop. She hadn't noticed the men racing towards her. Taking a Swiss Army knife out of her pocket, she used one of the blades to clean the tongue slime from under her nails. She tossed the brownish-pink glop to the ground with a flick, working diligently on the next nail, but that concentration was shattered when the others arrived.

    Surrounded by wheezing mountains of comatose geckos, Shaw hugged Cassandra, and Dillon held Riley so hard she dropped the knife. Laughing, crying, and throwing out questions, the happiness over this delightful reunion could not last. Dillon raised his voice.

"We are not sure what's really happening, and there may be more out there, and we don't know if these things will come back to life or not. Let's go back to the mall right now!"

President Cadwell had felt awful when he'd ordered the military presence in Vero Beach to withdraw, but the popular support of the Pink Legion and Melissa's marriage to his own brother had tied his hands like a puppet on a string. Those days were over. He was about to send the soldiers back to Vero, even if that meant he'd lose the next election. Humans can't be used as nutrition for those mutated geckos any longer. He was about to call the general, but his assistant told him about another option.

Ashinka was a small country bordering Nepal and China. Their ambassador had come to the White House that morning with a plan to stop the massacre on the Florida coast. Cadwell invited Ambassador Zhamian into his office, and they shook hands and bowed. The emissary placed his briefcase on the table between them.

"Our meeting may be fortuitous for both of us," President Cadwell said. "I was about to use our own military for the second time, but your scientists have come up with an easier option. I have not even thought over the problem of thousands of gecko bodies piling up and how we'd handle that."

Zhamian bowed and opened his briefcase. "We are blessed you will consider our request." He placed some papers in front of Cadwell. "We have found a way to stop the geckos. Please look this over. Perhaps impossible on paper, it is real. Liege Rimchi will explain more to you in the phone call. We can save your citizens and ourselves with the same action."

Setting up a direct call to the Liege, the President's assistant, and the ambassador himself would stay in the office to help with any confusion in the conversation.

"Good afternoon. Is this Liege Rimchi?"

"Wonderful to speak to you, President Cadwell."

"We will find the resolution. Zhamian has not expanded completely on your idea. Please, tell me more."

"We can stop the lizards without killing them. At least, not right away. We will use their flesh to end the starvation in our country. When their bodies reach Ashinka, it will be like rain after a drought. When I heard about the attacks on your own citizens, I think this answer has wider parameters."

"I attempted to stop the slaughter as soon as it began," the president said, lowering his voice. "But circumstances stalled my first attempt." And then his voice got louder with a ring of confidence. "Your technology shall be part of the answer. We will end this travesty."

The Liege responded, "Together, we'll undercut the support for the geckos by describing the violent murders of your citizens, and in our project, we'll end starvation in Ashinka. That should be enough to rally your people to the new cause." He shook his head. "Those devils would have just kept on without any interference!"

President Cadwell was excited. "Americans won't be attacked and eaten anymore!"

The control the Pink Legion had over him was gone.

The organizers of The Pink Legion, Caitlyn and Melissa, waited for their flight to Colorado out of the Washington Reagon National Airport in DC. They believed they had protected a new species birthed in Vero Beach, a real triumph for the Legion and a feather in their hats. This was a well-deserved vacation in a spa hidden in the Colorado mountains.

Melissa stared at the television screen. CNN was on. CNN was always on in every airport in the United States; homogenized news was thrown at audiences unable to change the channel or leave the room. She hadn't been paying attention, but a story snagged her like a hook, baited with vexation.

'*Yesterday, fifteen cargo ships anchored off the coast of Florida. One of our own reporters is there to investigate the …*'

"Caitlyn, wake up!" Melissa nudged her. "Something's going on!"

'*…helicopters from Ashinka are flying from the ships. It's happening live. These aircraft are dropping off dead or unconscious geckos on the large decks of these commercial vessels. We're not sure exactly what's going on, but this unusual process isn't stopping anytime soon. I assume Ashinka have a real interest in….*"

Caitlyn sat up and looked at the news. She quickly exploded. "What's going on in Vero Beach!"

People passing on the concourse stared at her, and a woman in the waiting area picked up her daughter and moved farther away. The news story went on.

Ashinka arranged a contract with President Cadwell to end the killing of defenseless Floridians. The extended drought that had destroyed Ashinka's crops is starving the population of that country. Shipping the gecko bodies to them would give them a new lease on life. We have an interview with the ambassador from Ashinka coming up in about….'

Caitlyn turned pink, barking high-pitched orders out to Melissa. "Get on the phone with your husband. Tell him to fix this thing right now!"

"I can't do that, Cat. Another country is now involved. There's nothing he can do." Melissa's pale face was another traumatic reaction against her companion's crimson flush.

'President Cadwell will address the nation at 7PM this evening and explain the situation. We have a good source that may give us more...'

Caitlyn couldn't take it anymore, and she ran to the restrooms. Melissa called out, "Stop! Our flight is boarding. We have to get on the plane."

She kept on running. The Pink Legion's triumph was dashed, and the miracle species was destroyed. Devasted, heartbroken, and furious, Caitlyn seethed over President Cadwell's actions. He was erasing this heavenly wonder!

General Hudson called Major Gordon to reenergize part of their military interactions in Vero Beach. They would help Ashinka airlift the geckos out of the city. The media's standpoint had changed as the Liege had predicted. News channels ran clips of starving villagers waiting for salvation from Florida. It became a heartwarming story retold through newspapers, magazines, and even across the web.

In a few days, the General looked at satellite feed over Vero Beach. The geckos were almost gone. In twelve more hours, he'd order the tanks to leave and open the borders.

Two cargo ships filled with lizards started the long trek to Paradip, a port on the coast of India. From there, the comatose geckos would be trucked to warehouses in Ashinka set up to care for them. The hunger plaguing the country should, theoretically, abate.

Major Gordan ordered twenty jeeps into Vero. He wasn't sure if every house had gotten the updated news. The jeep drivers would drive around with megaphones and announce that the danger was over. Gordan was concerned high wires and antennas could have been ripped out or knocked over by the hungry giants stamping around town.

Parking his jeep in front of the main entrance of Indian River Mall, people heard the jeep pull up, and many were drawn outside to hear what the soldier had to say. The lizards were almost gone.

He took his helmet off, giving the growing crowd more information. There was a touch of raspiness in his words, knowing the trauma they'd gone through...but he had to get back to work. The soldier got back in his jeep to touch more survivors hunkered out there.

Gus wanted to scope the city out, inviting Oliver to come along. Bringing guns in case of a possible straggler, they drove east to cross the Alma Lee Loy Bridge. They parked at the public beach and stepped out on the sand. Twelve cargo ships were still anchored out there. Suddenly, something flew right over their heads.

"That copter is moving fast, and it's holding a pallet with a gecko on it." Gus was excited. They watched as the helicopter reached one of the ships.

Taking binoculars out of his shoulder bag, Oliver watched what was happening out there. "The copter lowered the pallet onto the deck, and someone else used a forklift to put the lizard on a metal panel on the deck. An elevator of some kind dropped the animal below deck...now that helicopter is coming back. To get another one, I guess."

The wind had gotten strong enough to throw sand at their legs, but the heavier chop out there had not stopped the process.

"They're handling that breeze okay," Oliver said.

Two more copters passed, holding a larger support between them.

"Had to be an Agama."

"Yup. What was the name of the country helping us out?" Gus asked. "Was it Ashanga?"

"It's Ashinka."

The two men stayed at the beach for another hour to watch their nightmare disappear.

Three months after the giants were gone, the residents of Vero Beach tried to live their lives. The Police Chief and what was left of the City Council members came up with a tribute to remember the victims. Their bodies were digested and lost, so the officials arranged a memorial at the local airport. What was gone was not forgotten.

They bought a bronze plaque and inscribed it with the names of the departed using part of the donation money given to the town. Embedding the plaque in a slab of polished granite, they left it under the branches of a Northern Red Oak near the main building at the airport.

The day of the event was crisp and clear. The stage and stands had been erected near the airfield. Shaw and Dillon wore their Class A uniforms used for ceremonies and funerals, dark green with black stripes on the pant legs. There were black ribbons on their shields.

By the time Dillon and Shaw got there, the parking lot was full. They found a place to park on 26th, on a small road that passed the airport, and they had to walk to the stage.

"How are you and Riley doing? I can't believe things are getting close to normal."

A ghost of a smile, Dillon looked sideways at him. "*Normal?* I don't think so. The real estate market is on fire, that's true, and our houses are like gold, odd as that may be, yet it's still deserted around here—more like haunted. The emptiness creeps me out. How Vero became a magnet is a mystery to me…oh, I'm sorry. You asked about Riley. We're doing okay, even if memories drag on us sometimes."

"I got you. It's not easy to relax. Have you seen regular geckos reappearing? Some people are killing them, afraid they'll grow huge again. And did you hear about NASA's investigation to figure out what had started the whole thing?"

"I haven't heard a thing. Let me know if they figure it out."

They reached the stage and found some seats with the other officers. The Sheriff began the memorial with a speech. After that, Reverand John Vacchiano sermonized on loss and the process of healing. Eight Navy jets streaked across the sky in the form of a cross before veering off into an aerial ballet. The sorrow in many of the mourners was lifting as if the ceremony was like a bridge away from the isolation anchoring them down. A spiritual adieu to allow them to start up their lives again with lighter weight. The guilt they felt lived through the misfortune was absolved.

When Liege Rimchi heard about humans being eaten in Vero Beach, he told his scientists to find a way to stop the geckos. They came up with an answer. After the American president accepted his help, he revamped some factories in his own country to accept the lizards. The living bodies needed hydration and electrolytes in an intravenous system, and the workers got the last tube ready to insert into a gastrointestinal tract for the enteral nutrition they would also need… *just in time*. Countless geckos lived on their own individual platforms, able to survive indefinitely before being culled. Months or even years could pass.

Their meat would remain as fresh as if they'd been hunted down and shot the same day!

"Tender and Sweet," Ashinka's product undercut its competitors in pet food, imitation shellfish, and other fish products worldwide. Rimchi used low prices to support his apparent largesse, but his real motivations were less so. Sending glossy pamphlets out to a bevy of companies, they emphasized the fact that gecko flesh tastes better than cod. His personal bank account swelled like the heft of a hog at the trough while his own citizens' weight kept shrinking.

President Cadwell felt drained. The negotiations between India and Pakistan over trading laws affecting wild rice and curry shipped to the USA had been long and boring. Pakistan was still not done, insisting India had too many military bases on the border between them. Their negotiator insisted that the United States double the tax on anything India shipped to them before they dismantled two of those bases.

Nothing was decided, but at least it ended. Cadwell stood up and stretched, looking forward to having dinner with his wife. But she called. She had gotten a migraine, and he ended up alone in his private dining room.

Filet Mignon, a baked potato, and fresh asparagus. His mouth watered. Slathering butter on the potato, he sliced off a piece of meat and popped it into his mouth. Tender with perfect seasonings, it tasted heavenly… until his concern over the starvation in Ashinka intruded into his thoughts.

He'd call the Liege. Just ask him how things were going over there. He knew "Tender and Sweet" was doing well on the world market, making a bundle. He wondered if the people were growing their crops again? Is the starvation over? He rang a bell, and his assistant stepped over.

"Yes, Mr. President?"

"Connect me to Liege Rimchi's private line."

"Right away, sir."

The lanky young man placed an ancient-looking telephone in front of the president. Most of the phones in the white house were wired for security reasons. Too much surveillance was connected to the cells. Cadwell picked up the receiver and pushed a button. After some clattering, the connection went through.

"Hello, Liege Rimchi."

"Good evening, Mr. President. It is an honor to speak to you."

"Happy to have you on the line. I'm curious if the influx of food has helped your people? It was a boon for us, but has it worked for Ashinka?

"I understand your concern, President. We had been in a terrible state. Now, we rationed out protein to the needy, and I'm overseeing the recovery of our agricultural community. We shall return to farming again soon. Accepting our help gave us what we needed."

The president could hear someone interrupting the Liege.

"Please forgive me, President Cadwell. I must go. There is an open invitation to you to come here and enjoy the treasures in Ashinka whenever you like."

Cadwell's concern over Ashinka was gone. He ate the rest of his dinner. Right after dinner, a communications officer invited him to look at satellite images of the military bases on the Pakistan border in the control room on the first floor. President Cadwell followed the officer into the darkened room studded with lines of bright screens and technicians staring at them. He followed the officer...until he noticed a picture on one of the screens he'd seen before. The media used the same live image of a satellite orbiting Ashinka. A crowd huddled around an airport, starving. *It was still going on!* The relaxation on his face tightened. No point calling Rimchi back. The truth was in the pudding, and the pudding was rotten.

His parents were eaten. He raised his boot to stamp a three-inch-long gecko into a pancake, but it raced into a crack in the sidewalk. He walked onto a construction site to work for the company renovating a bungalow sold to a family from Ohio.

It had been half a year after the catastrophe. The population in Vero Beach had doubled as if those bloody weeks never happened. Like gigantic weeds, housing developments broke ground everywhere, and rentals and single homes didn't stay on the market for long. A long-term resident griped, "The place is turning into Fort Pierce!" And his companion rejoined, "Like a tea-cup version of Miami!"

Dillon had the day off. Riley was driving them out for errands in the Jeep. Stopped in the turning lane on 12th Street to get on Old Dixie Highway. When the arrow turned green, she swung through the intersection. The oncoming driver ignored their red light. Riley hadn't had enough time to hit the brakes, and the sedan kept speeding up, almost broadsiding them, happenchance their only savior.

"I'd turn on lights and sirens if I could!" She was badly rattled.

"It wouldn't matter. Seen any of those cop shows? That driver ignored a stop light, so there's a good chance they will ignore everything else. I deal with them every day, Riley. I stop them, I give them tickets, and sometimes drag them to jail, but nothing seems to affect their deadly driving habits."

She wanted to curse, sighing instead. "It used to be a breeze driving around here a few months ago."

Stopping at a cross street on Old Dixie to get on 14th Ave., a pickup truck barreled into the same lane she began to turn into from the opposite direction. This time, she hit the brakes, and the truck sailed past. Riley tightened the wheel.

"Relax, honey…please," Dillon spoke softly. "Relaaax." He touched her shoulder and planted a kiss on her cheek. "Crowded streets are always dangerous, and so far, no one has hit us. Hey, maybe we should pray to the traffic angels from now on. Pray in harmony as we leave the driveway next time." He sounded sincere, and she smiled.

"Could be a good idea. An arrow out of our own quiver shot up to management."

After buying a dish rack and a light sweater at the thrift store, their last stop was Publix. Dillon pushed the cart as Riley went through the list.

"It's past twelve, and I'm getting hungry. I feel like seafood salad. Do you want anything, Dillon?"

"Nope, I have leftover Chili from last night."

Three seafood salads were arranged at the fish counter. One was lobster and crab at sixteen dollars a pound. The next was cod, formed and dyed to look like lobster and crab stuffed into ugly-looking plastic squares for eight dollars. Riley liked the last one. Priced at five dollars for ten ounces, it was in some snazzy-looking containers that looked like scallop shells. She assumed the salad was also formed and dyed like the other one.

"This looks fine," Riley muttered to herself, not reading the ingredients. Ashinka's emblem on the label seemed familiar, but it hadn't registered hard enough. She was hungry. It was cheap. She'd try it out.

Getting home, they put the groceries away and sat down at the kitchen table — Dillon with his Chili and Riley with her fish salad. Liege Rimchi's prediction was coming true. There was a hint of the taste of cod in the gecko meat.

Riley swallowed a part of the leg muscle of the same Agama that had her rolled up in its tongue for lunch. After enjoying the tastiness of her salad, a gassy belch came out.

"Excuse me! I'm going to buy more of this salad." She had another bite. "They're using a good dressing on it!"

"Okay." But Dillon wasn't listening, instead reading the ingredients printed on the label of her seafood container. In his mind, that information should be replaced with more appropriate verification:

'In the end, what goes around comes around with a vengeance.'

Thank you for reading Everything in Vero Beach was Eaten.
Please post a review for the author on Amazon.com

Coming Soon

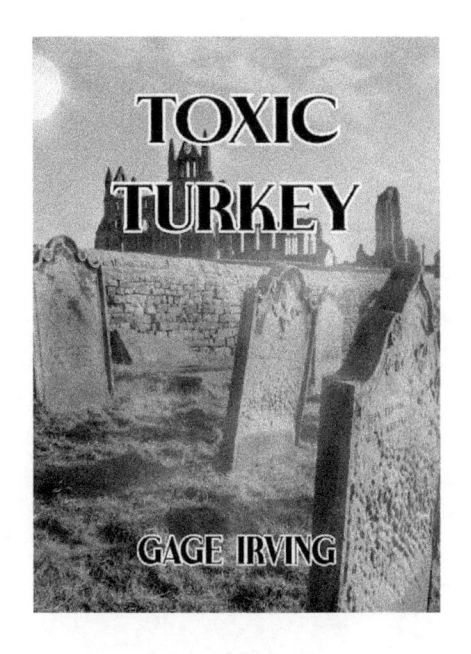

TOXIC TURKEY

GAGE IRVING

Also Coming

Toxic Tinsel
&
Devil's Dilemma

Printed in the USA
CPSIA information can be obtained
at www.ICGtesting.com
LVHW021527211124
797037LV00014B/757